P9-CEA-826

To Papá, with me always. For making me a bookworm.
To Emma and Teo, for the days and nights with books.
To Santiago, for everything.
L.D.L

To my parents, Pablo and Silvia, for teaching me to read and travel.
C.A.

First American edition published in 2019 by

CROCODILE BOOKS
An imprint of Interlink Publishing Group, Inc.
46 Crosby Street, Northampton, MA 01060
www.interlinkbooks.com

Text copyright © Luciana De Luca, 2018, 2019
Illustrations copyright © Cynthia Alonso, 2018, 2019
English language translation copyright © Interlink Publishing, 2019
Published in Spanish by Periplo Ediciones, Argentina

Library of Congress Cataloging-in-Publication data available:
ISBN-13: 978-1-62371-938-8

Printed and bound in Korea

Luciana De Luca   Cynthia Alonso

The Reader

Crocodile Books, USA
An imprint of Interlink Publishing Group, Inc.
www.interlinkbooks.com

The day begins on tiptoes,
in tiny whispers, as I climb down the stairs.

Upstairs, my parents are still asleep.
I would rather explore than sleep.

At this time of day, I am the owner of the house,
which happily opens its corners to me.

The library is almost always a little bit dark.
The rays of sunlight coming through the window
form a golden hopscotch on the floor.

Outside I can hear the chirping of cicadas.
They sing lullabies to the hot summer. In winter,
the chorus of the swaying trees comes through the
cracks in the window.

My parents always say, "You can read all the books
you can reach."

There are books that come up to my belly button
and books that come up to my shoulders.
Some are curiously placed just where the tips of my
fingers can reach. As I grow taller, I'll reach more
shelves and more books.

Some books have lots of pictures.
Others are very serious: the words,
like ants, run across the pages.
Some books are long and mysterious.
Others are light and fast.
Some are like vines holding me tight.
Others, like the wind, carry me far away.

Outside, some kids ride their bicycles while
a train thunders past, shaking the earth.
Others play hide and seek,
or just run around.

I choose a book, and then another.
And I read.

Reading takes me to places I have never been.
Places where no one is hungry, and you can
eat dessert for every meal.

Wild places where animals rule.

Underwater worlds, where
you never need to come
up for air.

Skies where you can nap in feathered clouds.

I read without stopping.
I am not distracted by anything.
Neither the laughter, nor the train, nor the pigeons
that walk on the clothesline where
the laundry hangs.

The more I read,
the bigger the world
becomes.

Wandering words move in and out of me.
I weave and unravel mysteries.

I travel without a passport or ticket.
I can find the way out of any maze.

I can be a giant,
or I can be invisible.

I can climb mountains or hide in
the earth, disguised as a seed.

Time is a hammock,
swaying me back...

...and forth.

And even when the words run out,
the story never ends...